Five Little Ducks

went swimming one day

Adapted by Russell Punter

Illustrated by Katya Longhi

5 little ducks went swimming one day,

over the hills and far away.

Mother Duck said,
"Quack, quack, quack, quack!"

But only **4** little ducks swam back.

4 little ducks went swimming one day,

over the hills and far away.

Mother Duck said,
"Quack, quack, quack, quack!"

But only **3** little ducks swam back.

3 little ducks went swimming one day,

over the hills and far away.

Mother Duck said,
    "Quack, quack, quack, quack!"

But only 2 little ducks swam back.

2 little ducks went swimming one day,
over the hills and far away.

Mother Duck said,
"Quack, quack, quack, quack!"

But only 1 little duck swam back.

1 little duck went swimming one day,

over the hills and far away.

Mother Duck said,

"Quack, quack, quack, quack!"

And all her 5 little ducks came back.

The first little duck swam up to say...

"I'm sorry I swam so far away.

I met a little dog who went **snip, snap!**

And that's when I came swimming back."

The second little duck swam up to say...

"I'm sorry I swam so far away.

I met a little fish who went **slip, slap!**

And that's when I came swimming back."

The third little duck swam up to say...

"I'm sorry I swam so far away.

I met a little bird who went
RAT- A- TAT- TAT!

And that's when I came
swimming back."

The fourth little duck swam up to say...

"I'm sorry I swam so far away.

I heard a scary **THUNDER CLAP!**

And that's when I came swimming back."

The fifth little duck swam up to say...

"I'm sorry I swam so far away.

I met a little bat who went *flip, flap!*

And that's when I came swimming back."

They all snuggle down and say, "Quack, quack.
We're so very glad that we came back."

Designed by Laura Nelson Norris

Edited by Lesley Sims

This edition first published in 2023 by Usborne Publishing Ltd.,83-85 Saffron Hill, London EC1N 8RT, England.
usborne.com Copyright © 2023, 2021 Usborne Publishing Ltd.